This Walker book belongs to:

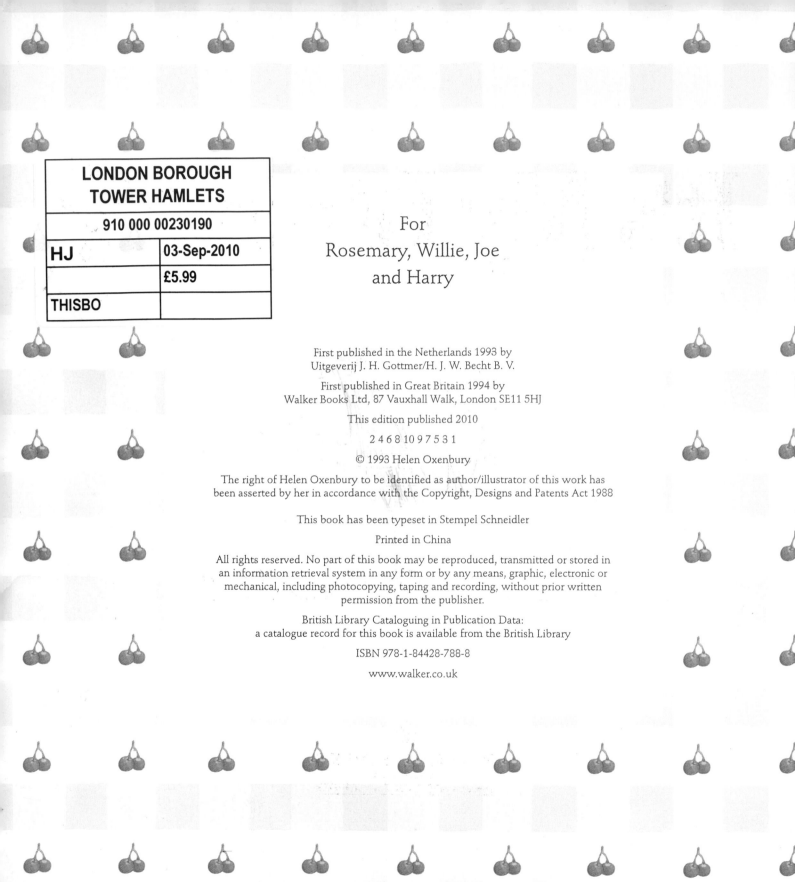

For
Rosemary, Willie, Joe
and Harry

First published in the Netherlands 1993 by
Uitgeverij J. H. Gottmer/H. J. W. Becht B. V.

First published in Great Britain 1994 by
Walker Books Ltd, 87 Vauxhall Walk, London SE11 5HJ

This edition published 2010

2 4 6 8 10 9 7 5 3 1

© 1993 Helen Oxenbury

The right of Helen Oxenbury to be identified as author/illustrator of this work has
been asserted by her in accordance with the Copyright, Designs and Patents Act 1988

This book has been typeset in Stempel Schneidler

Printed in China

British Library Cataloguing in Publication Data:
a catalogue record for this book is available from the British Library

ISBN 978-1-84428-788-8

www.walker.co.uk

It's My Birthday

HELEN OXENBURY

WALKER BOOKS
AND SUBSIDIARIES
LONDON • BOSTON • SYDNEY • AUCKLAND

"It's my birthday and
I'm going to make a cake."

"It's my birthday and
   I'm going to make a cake.
   I need some eggs."

"I'll get you some eggs,"
   said the chicken.

"It's my birthday and
 I'm going to make a cake.
 I've got the eggs.
 But I need some flour."

"I'll get you some flour,"
said the bear.

"It's my birthday and
   I'm going to make a cake.
   I've got the eggs and the flour.
   But I need some butter and milk."

"I'll get you some butter and milk,"
                said the cat.

"It's my birthday and
    I'm going to make a cake.
    I've got eggs, flour, butter and milk.
    But I need a pinch of salt."

"I'll get you a pinch of salt,"
                said the pig.

"It's my birthday and
I'm going to make a cake.
I've got eggs, flour, butter, milk
and a pinch of salt.
But I need some sugar."

"I'll get you some sugar,"
said the dog.

"It's my birthday and
   I'm going to make a cake.
   I've got eggs, flour, butter,
   milk, a pinch of salt, and sugar.
   But I need some cherries
   for the top."

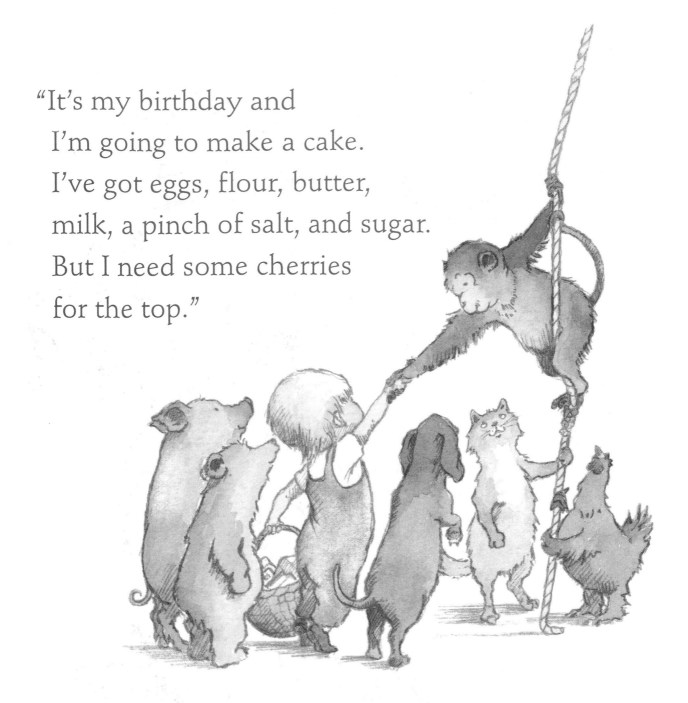

"I'll get you some cherries for the top,"
                    said the monkey.

"It's my birthday and
  I'm going to make a cake.
  I've got everything I need."

"We'll all help you make the cake,"
  said the chicken, the bear,
  the cat, the pig, the dog
  and the monkey.

"Thank you, everybody.
Now all of you can …

...help me eat the cake!"

"Happy Birthday!"

More books by Helen Oxenbury:

Mem Fox   Helen Oxenbury
Ten Little Fingers and Ten Little Toes

ISBN 978-1-4063-1956-9

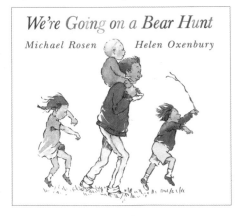

We're Going on a Bear Hunt
Michael Rosen   Helen Oxenbury

ISBN 978-0-7445-2323-2

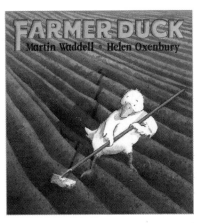

FARMER DUCK
Martin Waddell · Helen Oxenbury

ISBN 978-0-7445-3660-7

Available from all good bookstores
www.walker.co.uk